Look for the **Scooby-Doo Mysteries**.
Collect them all!

Written by
James Gelsey

A
LITTLE APPLE
PAPERBACK

SCHOLASTIC INC.

New York Toronto London Auckland Sydney
Mexico City New Delhi Hong Kong

For Jules and Rose

No part of this work may be reproduced, stored in a retrieval system, or transmitted in any form or by any means, electronic, mechanical, photocopying, recording, or otherwise, without written permission of the publisher. For information regarding permission, write to Scholastic Inc., Attention: Permissions Department, 555 Broadway, New York, NY 10012.

ISBN 0-439-18877-6

12 11 10   3 4 5/0

Printed in the U.S.A.
First Scholastic printing, November 2000

Chapter 1

"Easy does it, Scoob," Shaggy said. He and Scooby were sitting in the back of the Mystery Machine. They were stacking empty chocolate pudding cups on top of one another.

"Just one more and our tower will be complete," Shaggy said proudly.

Scooby was about to put the last cup on top. Then the Mystery Machine made a sharp turn.

"Ruh-roh!" Scooby barked as he lost his balance. He fell right on top of the tower. The cups rolled all over the floor of the van.

"Rawwwwwww," Scooby sighed.

"Don't be sad, Scoob," Shaggy said. "It's like my mother used to say: No use crying over spilled chocolate pudding cups."

He and Scooby giggled.

"Sorry about that sudden turn," Fred called back. "Someone nearly cut us off. But we're here now."

"Like, where's here?" Shaggy asked.

"Howard's," Daphne replied.

"Who's Howard?" Shaggy asked.

"Howard's is not a who," Velma replied. "It's a what."

"I don't know," Shaggy said. "Like, that's why I'm asking you."

"Howard's is a department store, Shaggy," Daphne said. "We came to buy some birthday presents, remember?"

"Right," Shaggy said. "Whose birthday is it?"

"Yours," Velma replied.

"But my birthday was last week," Shaggy said.

"No, it wasn't," Velma said.

"Sure it was," Shaggy said. "Scooby and I were at the pizza parlor. We told the pizza guy it was my birthday so we could get a free pizza."

"Shaggy, you always tell the pizza guy it's your birthday so you can get a free pizza," Daphne said. "That doesn't make it your real birthday."

"I guess I've used that line so many times," Shaggy said, "I've forgotten when my birthday really is."

"Well, we haven't," Fred said.

"That's what friends are for," Daphne said.

"So, like, what are you going to buy me?" Shaggy asked.

"It's a surprise," Velma said.

"And it won't be anything if we spend all afternoon sitting in the van," Fred said. "Let's go."

The gang got out of the van and walked across the parking lot. They saw a big gray truck parked right outside the store. The truck's back door was wide open. "Filbert's Security Systems," Daphne read off the side of the truck.

"I'd say this is one security system that could use a few pointers," Velma said.

"And what kind of pointers do you mean, young lady?" a man asked.

The gang looked over and saw a man standing by the other side of the truck. He wore a long white lab coat.

"Just that leaving a security truck un-locked and open like this isn't very secure," Velma replied.

"That's only because I haven't activated the security system," the man replied. "I'm

Dr. Filbert, and this is one of my newest inventions."

The man took a small remote control device out of his coat pocket. He pushed a button and waited. He pushed the button again and again. Then he banged the remote control against his hand a couple of times.

"Oh, dear. Please excuse me." Dr. Filbert climbed up into the back of the truck. He closed the doors behind him.

"That was rather odd," Velma said.

"Like, let's not waste any more time," Shaggy said. "You have presents to buy." He gently pushed the others up the sidewalk and into the store.

Chapter 2

The gang walked inside Howard's department store and looked around. The place was enormous.

"I forgot how big this place is," Daphne said.

"Not only is it the biggest department store in the whole state," Velma reminded her, "it's also the oldest."

"Okay, Shaggy," Daphne said. "If your present is going to be a surprise, you can't walk around with us."

"Like, that's okay," Shaggy said. "Me and Scoob will check out the cooking department. You never know when they're gonna give out free samples, right, Scoob?"

"Reah, ree ramples!" Scooby barked.

"You can ask that stock clerk over there for directions," Fred said.

Shaggy and Scooby walked over to a stock clerk standing on a ladder. He was trying to hang a SALE sign from the ceiling.

"Like, excuse us," Shaggy said. The clerk suddenly lost his balance and *CRASH*! He fell right off the ladder and into a box of socks and sweaters.

"Hey, are you all right?" Shaggy asked, reaching out to help the clerk.

The clerk sat up and shook his head.

"I think so," he said. "Good thing I wasn't next to the pins and needles display." He carefully climbed out of the box. Fred, Daphne, and Velma ran over.

"Shaggy, what did you do?" Velma asked.

"Like, nothing," Shaggy said.

"It wasn't his fault," the clerk said. "My

foot must have slipped or something."

"What's going on over there?" someone yelled. A tall man in a security uniform ran over to them.

"Everything's okay, Josh," the clerk said.

"What happened, Artie?" the man said.

"I was hanging the sign and I lost my balance is all," the clerk replied. "I'm okay. These nice folks came over to help me."

"Josh Lester, store security," the man told

the gang. "I'm sorry if this caused any inconvenience to your shopping experience."

"That's all right," Daphne said. "It was sort of our fault."

"No, it was all my fault," Artie, the clerk, said.

"Well, we'll take care of it from here," Josh said. "You folks have a pleasant day."

"Now let's go find that cooking department, Scoob," Shaggy said. "All this excitement has made me hungry."

Shaggy and Scooby turned and walked right into something. It was a giant robot.

"Zoinks!" Shaggy exclaimed.

"Rikes!" Scooby barked as he jumped into Shaggy's arms.

9

"What in the world is that?" Josh exclaimed.

The robot walked right up to the clerk. The robot grabbed Artie's leg and lifted him up into the air. Artie's head and arms dangled over the floor while the robot made a sound like a siren.

"Help! Help me!" Artie screamed. A small crowd gathered around to see what was happening.

A moment later, Dr. Filbert appeared. He ran over to the robot and Artie.

"Very good, robot," he said. He took the remote control from his pocket and pushed a button. The siren stopped.

"My goodness!" a woman said as she pushed her way through the crowd. "What on earth is going on?"

"Mrs. Howard!" Josh exclaimed. "What are you doing down here?"

"I'm here to see what's upsetting all of my customers," Mrs. Howard replied. "Dr. Filbert, would you mind telling me what's happening? And please tell your robot to put Artie down."

Dr. Filbert pushed a few buttons on his remote control. The robot lowered Artie back to the floor.

"Ladies and gentlemen," Mrs. Howard addressed the crowd. "I am so sorry for this disturbance. We at Howard's want you to have a pleasant shopping experience. So to make up for it, we will take fifteen percent off every purchase for the next fifteen minutes."

The crowd quickly dispersed as people ran through the store.

"Now, Dr. Filbert, you have some explaining to do," Mrs. Howard said sternly.

Chapter 3

"**Y**ou told me you fixed all of the problems with your Super Security Device, Dr. Filbert," Mrs. Howard continued.

"Super Security Device?" Josh said. "You mean he's supposed to do my job?"

"Now, Josh," Mrs. Howard said. "You have to admit you are getting close to retirement age."

"But to replace me with a bucket of bolts?" Josh asked.

"The SSD-Three is not a bucket of bolts," Dr. Filbert said. "It is a remote-controlled

Super Security Device that never needs a coffee break and never makes a mistake."

"Except for today," Velma whispered.

"Not so fast, young lady," Dr. Filbert said. "The SSD-Three must have detected some criminal behavior."

"All I did was fall off the ladder in a pile of socks," Artie explained. "I didn't steal anything."

"Excuse me, Artie," Josh said. "But what's that in your pocket?" Josh pointed to a small lump in the pocket of Artie's pants. Artie reached into the pocket. He blushed as he pulled out a sock.

"Aha!" Dr. Filbert said. "So you did steal something. See, the SSD-Three was right!"

"But I didn't steal it," Artie said. "They must've ended up in there when I fell into the pile."

"And that's something a real security guard would understand," Josh added.

"Dr. Filbert, I won't pay you another penny until this robot is working flawlessly," Mrs. Howard stated. "Until then, I want you and your robot out of my store."

Artie and Josh smiled at each other.

"Artie, this is all your fault," Mrs. Howard continued. "If you weren't so clumsy, none of this would have happened. Now clean up this mess." Mrs. Howard walked past the gang. "Only ten minutes left for that fifteen percent discount, you know," she told them.

"Do you need any help cleaning up, Artie?" Daphne asked.

"No, thanks," he replied. "I'll be fine. But

if I see that robot again, I don't know what I'll do."

"I know what you mean, Artie," Josh said. "Here, let me give you a hand."

The gang watched as Josh and Artie started straightening up.

"We'll meet up with you and Scooby as soon as we can, Shaggy," Daphne said.

"Like, take your time," Shaggy replied. "I wouldn't want you to feel rushed in picking out my present."

"We're not worried about needing time to pick out your present," Velma said. "We're worried about giving you and Scooby too much time to get into trouble."

"Now what kind of trouble could we get into here?" Shaggy asked.

"I don't know, but you'll find some way," Fred said. "So just be careful."

Fred, Velma, and Daphne walked farther into the store until Shaggy and Scooby lost sight of them.

"All right, Scoob, we're on our own," Shaggy said, looking around. "Hmm, I wonder which way it is to the cooking section."

Scooby lifted his nose into the air and took a few deep sniffs. Then he put his nose to the floor and smelled all around.

"Rollow re," Scooby said. He followed a scent along the floor with Shaggy close behind.

"To the kitchens!" Shaggy called.

"Ruh ritchens!" Scooby echoed.

Chapter 4

Shaggy and Scooby stepped onto the *down* escalator.

"Scoob, are you sure this is the way?" Shaggy asked. "Like, I feel like we've ridden this escalator about sixty times."

"Wheeeeeeee!" Scooby called. He was sliding down the banister.

"You're just doing this for fun, aren't you, Scoob?" Shaggy asked. "Zoinks! L-l-look at that!"

As Shaggy and Scooby rode down the escalator, they saw the security robot ride up on the other side.

"Like, I can't believe that robot's back," Shaggy said. He and Scooby got off the escalator at the bottom.

"Rone rore rime!" Scooby barked. He jumped onto the *up* escalator.

"Oh, no you don't," Shaggy said. "I'm not going up there with that creepy robot walking around."

Scooby faced Shaggy as he rode up the escalator. He waved his front paw.

"Rye, Raggy," Scooby barked.

Shaggy watched Scooby ride all the way to the top.

"All right, Scooby, you had your fun!" called Shaggy. "Now come on back down!"

Shaggy waited, but Scooby didn't come back down.

"Scooby-Doo?" Shaggy called. "Man, like I hope that robot didn't get him," he muttered. "Hang on, Scooby, I'll save you!"

Shaggy jumped onto the escalator and

ran all the way to the top.

"Scooby-Doo, where are you?" Shaggy yelled.

"Right rere!" Scooby barked. He jumped up behind Shaggy and gave him a big Scooby hug.

"Hey, cut that out!" Shaggy said. "How are we ever going to find the food if you keep playing around? Now let's go."

Shaggy and Scooby walked through the shoe department, past the hand-bags, and around the dresses.

"Hey look, it's the robot again," Shaggy whispered to Scooby. They watched the robot walk into the hardware department. The robot stopped in front of a tool display. It looked around to see if anyone was watching, then gazed at the tools. It reached out and pulled something off the rack. The robot looked around again and this time spotted Shaggy and Scooby.

"Zoinks! He saw us!" Shaggy exclaimed. "Let's get out of here!"

The robot started walking toward them. It took big robot steps. Shaggy and Scooby ran back through the dress, handbag, and shoe departments. They hopped onto the *down* escalator. The robot ran onto the escalator after them. All the other customers jumped out of their way.

Halfway down, Shaggy said, "Let's give him the slip, Scoob." Shaggy jumped over the handrail from the *down* to the *up* escalator. The robot reached out to grab Scooby's tail. Scooby managed to jump over the handrail just in time.

"Good move, Scoob," Shaggy said. "Let's go!" He and Scooby ran all the way to the top. They watched the robot try to hop over the handrail. It lost its balance and fell over, bumping all the way to the bottom.

"Now let's go find the others and tell them what we saw," Shaggy said. "But this time we'll take the elevator."

Chapter 5

Shaggy and Scooby walked around the store looking for the rest of the gang.

"Fred! Daphne! Velma!" Shaggy called. "Like, where are you guys?"

Josh Lester, the security guard, looked up when he heard Shaggy's voice. He followed Shaggy's voice across the store until he caught up to Shaggy and Scooby.

"Excuse me, young man," Josh Lester said. "Mrs. Howard does not want people shouting in her store. It disturbs the other customers."

"I'll bet not as much as, like, a stealing ro-bot," Shaggy answered.

"What are you talking about?" asked Josh.

"Scoob and I saw that crazy security robot steal something from the tool department," Shaggy said. "When he saw us watching him, he started chasing us."

"Sounds to me like that robot's gone hay-wire," Josh responded. "I'll go check it out." Josh walked toward the escalator. As he went up, he passed Fred, Daphne, and Velma rid-ing down.

"There you are!" Shaggy called. "Like, it's time to go."

"Time to go?" Daphne asked. "But we still haven't found your present."

"Like, that's okay, Daph," Shaggy replied. "Your present to me can be us getting out of here."

"Why do you two want to leave all of a sudden?" Fred asked.

"Show 'em, Scoob," Shaggy said.

Scooby stood up on his hind legs. He started lurching around like a robot. Then he looked at Shaggy and pretended to chase him.

"I think you two spent too much time in the toy department," Daphne said.

"No, but that creepy robot spent too much time in the tool department," Shaggy said. "Scooby and I saw him steal something."

"Robots don't just steal things," Velma stated. "Especially security robots. I think you and Scooby just have overactive imaginations."

Suddenly, everyone heard the sound of glass breaking, followed by some shouts. A loud alarm rang throughout the store.

"That sounds like it's coming from the jewelry department," Fred said. "Let's go!"

The gang rushed across the store to the jewelry department. There they saw that one of the glass jewelry cases had been smashed. Mrs. Howard came running over.

"What happened here?" she asked with some panic in her voice.

A soft groan came from behind the jewelry counter. Fred looked and saw Artie sitting on the floor. He was holding his head.

Fred and Shaggy helped him up.

"What happened, Artie?" asked Mrs. Howard.

"You're not going to believe this," Artie replied. "I had just brought over a carton of jewelry boxes. Then that robot came over and smashed the glass. It grabbed a handful of jewels, knocked me down, and ran away."

"Who grabbed a handful of jewels?" Josh Lester asked as he ran over.

"Where have you been, Josh?" Mrs. Howard asked.

"There was a theft in the hardware department," Josh explained. "Someone stole a hammer."

"That's nothing," Artie said. "That stupid security robot came here and stole some jewelry."

"Actually, it didn't steal just any jewelry, Mrs. Howard," said Josh as he looked into the broken jewelry case. "All it took was the Wellington watch."

"Oh, dear!" Mrs. Howard looked as if she was about faint. Artie caught her arm and steadied her just in time.

"What's the Wellington watch?" Velma asked.

"It's the first item that Horatio Howard, the store's founder, stocked back in 1897," Moe said. "It's a family heirloom. It doesn't have much value, but it's pretty important to Mrs. Howard."

"And, like, now it's pretty gone," Shaggy whispered to Scooby.

"Shaggy!" scolded Daphne.

"Don't worry, Mrs. Howard," Fred said. "We'll get to the bottom of this."

"Oh, no you don't," Josh said. "I'm the head of security here. And I'm not going to be replaced by a robot or a bunch of kids. I'll take care of this myself, Mrs. Howard." Josh turned and walked away.

"Artie . . ." began Mrs. Howard.

"I know, I know," Artie said. "Clean up this mess and get back to work." Artie walked away sadly.

"I was just going to give him the afternoon off," Mrs. Howard said. "Anyway, kids, I don't care what Josh says. If you find that robot and the watch first, you'll get a very handsome reward."

As Mrs. Howard walked back to her office, the gang huddled together.

"The first thing we need to do is look for clues," Fred said. "Daphne and I will try to track down Dr. Filbert and ask him some questions about his robot."

"And Shaggy, Scooby, and I can look

around the jewelry department for clues," Velma said.

"Like, do we have to?" Shaggy asked.

"The sooner we solve this mystery, the sooner we can get back to shopping for your birthday present," Daphne said.

"And the sooner we can get out of here," added Fred.

"Like, don't just stand there," Shaggy said. "Let's get to work."

Chapter 6

Shaggy, Scooby, and Velma walked over to the smashed jewelry case. Broken glass was everywhere.

"Jinkies," Velma exclaimed. "That robot sure made a mess." As Velma carefully examined the jewelry case, something caught Scooby's attention.

"Raggy," whispered Scooby. "Rook!"

Shaggy looked over and saw a man wearing a white chef's hat and apron.

"Where there's a chef, you can bet there's food, Scoob," Shaggy whispered back. "You keep an eye on him, and I'll take care of Velma."

"Right," Scooby barked. He focused his eyes on the chef and watched his every move.

"Velma," Shaggy said, "Scooby and I, like, want to see if we can find some more clues."

"That's a first," Velma said. "Where do you want to look?"

"In the cooking — I mean the hardware department," Shaggy said. "Where we saw him earlier."

"That's actually not a bad idea, Shaggy," Velma said. "I'm glad to see you and Scooby have more on your minds than just food."

"Let's go, Scooby-Doo," Shaggy said. He and Scooby headed out of the jewelry department.

"So, which way to the food, Scoob?" asked Shaggy.

"Ris ray," Scooby barked.

The two buddies could see the top of the chef's hat just above the racks of clothing as they followed his path through the store. Shaggy and Scooby followed the hat through the coats, past the hats, just behind the perfumes, and into the cooking department. Then the hat seemed to disappear.

"Did we lose him?" Shaggy asked. "Like, chefs can't just vanish."

"Maybe he's hiding with that robot," Artie said. He was placing some pots and pans on the shelves.

"Like, where's that?" Shaggy asked.

"I don't know," replied Artie. "I just said that 'cause it seems like no one can find that robot. So it must have a pretty good hiding place. Anyway, that chef guy will be back soon. He's getting things ready for his next cooking demonstration."

"Like, thanks, man," Shaggy said. "Come on, Scoob, I guess we'd better get back to Velma."

"Don't bother," Velma said. Shaggy and Scooby turned around and saw Velma standing there.

"I thought you were looking for clues in the hardware section," Velma said. "What are you doing in the cooking department?"

"Like, what better place is there to satisfy our starving curiosity?" Shaggy asked with a smile.

"In any event, I'm glad I found you, Artie," Velma continued. "When you saw the robot smash the jewelry case, how did it do it?"

"I don't know," Artie replied. "I guess I was so surprised to see the robot, I didn't notice."

"Do you think it could have used this?" Velma asked. She showed Artie a small hammer. "I found this on the floor behind the jewelry counter."

"Hmm, look at that," said Artie. "Maybe it did use it."

"Shaggy, Scooby, let's go find Fred and Daphne," Velma said. "I think we're getting close to solving this case."

"We'll be right there, Velma," Shaggy said. "Psst, Artie," whispered Shaggy. "When did you say that chef guy would be back?"

"About five minutes," replied Artie. "Right over there."

"Thanks," Shaggy whispered. "Coming, Velma," he called to his mystery-loving friend.

Chapter 7

Velma saw Fred and Daphne riding up the escalator.

"Fred, Daphne!" Velma called. "Over here!"

The gang met in front of a big tent next to the sporting goods department.

"What were you doing on the second floor?" Velma asked.

"Dr. Filbert's security truck was still parked out front, but we couldn't find him anywhere," Daphne explained. "So we decided to check out the hardware department. What did you find?"

"Only this," Velma replied, showing them the hammer. "I think the robot used it to smash the jewelry case."

"But why would a robot need to use a hammer to break glass?" Fred asked.

"Like, so it doesn't ruin its robot manicure?" Shaggy suggested.

"Or so it doesn't get cut on the broken glass," Daphne added.

"Why would a robot care about getting cut?" Fred said.

"My thoughts exactly," Velma said. "I asked Artie, and he doesn't remember if the robot used the hammer or not."

"Well, one thing's for certain," Fred continued. "That's exactly the kind of hammer that was taken from the hardware department."

"Things are starting to

fall into place," Velma said. "It looks to me like this Super Security Device is really a Sloppy Stealing Device."

"Velma's right," Fred said. "It's time to set a trap. And I think I know just what to do. But we'll need Mrs. Howard's help."

"Velma and I will go talk to Mrs. Howard," Daphne said.

"And Shaggy, Scooby, and I will take care of everything else," Fred said.

"Hey, where are they?" Velma asked.

Fred, Daphne, and Velma looked around. Shaggy and Scooby were sneaking away.

"Hold on there, you two," Daphne called. "Just where do you think you're going?"

"Rooking department," Scooby barked.

"Scoob means 'looking' department," Shaggy said. "Like, as in, we're looking for clues, right, Scoob?"

"Reah, rues," Scooby agreed.

"You're going to the cooking department for that demonstration, aren't you?" Velma asked.

"There's no time for that now, fellas," Fred said. "We need your help if we're going to catch that robot."

"Like, no way," Shaggy said. "Scooby-Doo and I have had enough robot running around to last us a while."

"Hey, Scoob," Daphne sang. "Would you help us out for a Scooby Snack?"

Scooby looked at Shaggy. Shaggy shook his head.

"Ruh-ruh," Scooby said, shaking his head like Shaggy.

"How about two Scooby Snacks?" Velma asked.

Scooby looked at Shaggy. Shaggy shook his head again.

"Ruh-ruh," Scooby said, also shaking his head.

"Three?" Daphne asked.

Scooby looked at Shaggy again. Shaggy shook his head no for a third time.

Scooby thought for a moment, then nodded up and down. "Rokay!" he barked.

Daphne reached into her bag and pulled out a box of Scooby Snacks. She tossed three into the air. Scooby jumped up and gobbled them down.

"Ranks!" barked Scooby.

"Sold out for three Scooby Snacks," moaned Shaggy. "Okay, Fred, what do you want us to do?"

"Listen carefully," Fred began.

Chapter 8

"Here's what we know so far," Fred said. "We know that the robot must be around because Dr. Filbert's van is still here."

"We also know that the robot must be trying to get back at Mrs. Howard for something," Daphne added. "Otherwise, it would have stolen something a lot more valuable than an old watch."

"So let's make it think that Mrs. Howard isn't really bothered by it," Velma suggested.

"We'll get her to make a storewide announcement about the robot," said Fred. "The robot will be sure to come out."

"And let me guess," Shaggy said. "Like, that's where Scooby and I come in."

"Right," Fred agreed. "The important thing is to trap the robot somewhere where it can't hide or escape. So Scooby will lure the robot into this tent. When the robot's inside, Shaggy and I will zip up the tent."

"But what happens to Scooby?" Shaggy asked.

"He can slip out through the window flap in the back," Fred answered. "Now let's get started."

Daphne and Velma went to get Mrs. Howard. Fred walked around the outside of the tent.

"Hmm, I think we could use a little rope, just in case," Fred said. "I'll go get some from the hardware department. You two wait here." Fred walked toward the *down* escalator.

Shaggy and Scooby looked at each other.

"You know, Scoob," Shaggy said. "I'll bet

that the chef is right in the middle of his cooking demonstration. You know what that means?"

"Ree ramples!" Scooby barked.

Shaggy and Scooby walked as fast as they could toward the cooking department.

"Attention, Howard's shoppers!" Mrs. Howard's voice filled the department store. "Our robot promotion is now over. No more robots will be around to upset your shopping experience. Thank you for shopping at Howard's, and have a good day."

"We'd better grab our free snacks and hurry back to the tent," Shaggy said. He and Scooby walked up to the demonstration kitchen. A tall man in a chef's hat and apron stood with his back to them.

"Excuse us, Mr. Chef, sir," Shaggy said.

"Like, what's cooking in the kitchen?"

The chef turned around.

"Zoinks!" Shaggy exclaimed.

"Rikes!" Scooby barked.

"Robot!" they yelled together.

The chef was really the runaway robot dressed in a chef's hat and apron!

"Run, Scoob!" Shaggy shouted. They turned and ran through the maze of displays. The robot was close behind.

"Let's split up, Scoob," Shaggy called. "I'll run back to the tent and find Fred. You keep that robot busy for a few minutes." Shaggy then made a quick turn and disappeared

down an aisle. The robot kept following Scooby.

Just past the luggage department, Scooby looked over his shoulder. The robot was gone.

"Rhew!" Scooby gasped. Then Scooby faced forward again.

"Rikes!" he yelped. The robot stood at the end of the aisle in front of him. Scooby ran right between the robot's legs.

"To the tent, Scoob!" Shaggy yelled. "This way!" Scooby ran toward Shaggy's voice. He saw Shaggy and Fred standing next to the tent. Scooby tried to run faster, but he lost his footing. He slid along the slippery floor right past the tent and into a mannequin. The mannequin toppled over. The robot couldn't stop in time and tripped over the mannequin. The robot sailed through the air and landed with a thud in a big box of woollen socks. Scooby raced over and jumped on top of the robot.

Chapter 9

"You did it, Scoob!" Shaggy said. "Nice work, Scooby," Fred said.

Velma, Daphne, and Mrs. Howard came running over.

"Nicely done, children," Mrs. Howard said. "Now I'd like to see who's behind all this."

"Be our guest, Mrs. Howard," Fred said. He stepped aside, and Mrs. Howard walked up to the robot. She reached out and tried to take off its head.

"Owwwww!" came a voice from inside. "That hurts!"

"I didn't know robots could talk," Shaggy said.

"It's not really a robot, Shaggy," Daphne whispered.

"Oh, yeah, like, I knew that," Shaggy said.

The robot reached up and gave its head a half twist. Then it lifted off its head.

"Artie!" Mrs. Howard exclaimed. "You're the robot?"

"Just as we thought," said Velma.

"How could you possibly have known?" Mrs. Howard asked.

"Known what?" Josh Lester asked as he walked over. He was with Dr. Filbert.

"Known that our runaway robot was really Artie in disguise," Mrs. Howard replied. "And where have you been all this time, Dr. Filbert?"

"I was in the store's computer center, trying to work out the kinks in the SSD-Three," Dr. Filbert answered. "I know you told me to leave the store, but I needed access to some high-speed computers. I didn't think you'd mind."

"And you call yourself a security guard, Josh?" Mrs. Howard asked. "How could you let Dr. Filbert gain access to our computer center?"

"Actually, you gave Dr. Filbert access," Josh answered. "When you hired him, you gave him access to our entire store so he could develop the right kind of security system for us."

"Which is why he was our first suspect," Velma put in. "We figured he would know all about the store's ins and outs. That would explain how the robot could appear and disappear so easily."

"Dr. Filbert also had a reason to get back at you, Mrs. Howard," Daphne continued.

"After all, you did tell him you weren't going to pay him anymore."

"But I would never want my SSD-Three to get a reputation for stealing," Dr. Filbert said. "That would be wrong."

"So that left Artie and Josh Lester," said Fred.

"Me?" Josh asked, surprised. "How could you think I would do this?"

"Because you didn't want to lose your job to a robot," Velma explained. "You said so yourself. It stands to reason that you'd want to get back at Mrs. Howard."

"But then we checked out the hardware department," Daphne continued. "The clerk told us he saw you there after the hammer was stolen."

"Thanks to that tip from your friend and his dog," added Josh.

"You were there at exactly the same time that the robot stole the Wellington watch," Fred said. "So that ruled you out."

"Which left Artie," Velma said. "And we almost believed that he really did see the robot steal the watch."

"But then we found this hammer hidden behind the jewelry case," Daphne explained.

"A robot wouldn't need a hammer to break glass," Fred said.

"Of course," Mrs. Howard said. "Only a person would use a hammer so he wouldn't get cut. So you lied about seeing the robot steal the watch, Artie. Why?"

"Because I was mad at it and at you," Artie said. "First that stupid robot embarrassed me in front of the entire store. Then *you* embarrassed me in front of the entire store. 'This is all your fault, Artie.' Talking to me like I was some little nobody, in front of all those people."

"I was upset that you had caused such a scene. And I was talking to you like you were a stock clerk in my department store," Mrs. Howard responded.

"Well, I was sick of being talked to like I was a klutz, okay? So I decided to teach you all a lesson. If my plan had worked, that robot would have been history. And after I scared away enough customers, so would you and this store."

"Josh, take him away," Mrs. Howard said. Josh helped Artie off the sock display. "But first, I think he owes me something."

Mrs. Howard held out her hand. Artie reached inside the robot suit. His hand came out holding the Wellington watch. Then Josh handcuffed Artie and led him away.

"What I don't understand," Mrs. Howard said, "is where he got the robot suit to begin with."

"That was my fault," Dr. Filbert said. "I was having difficulties with the remote locking mechanism on my truck. Artie must have

gotten inside when the truck was open. He very easily could have taken parts of the SSD-One or SSD-Two models I had in there. I'm very sorry, Mrs. Howard."

"That's all right, Dr. Filbert," Mrs. Howard said. She turned to Scooby. "And as for you kids, name your reward. Anything in the store."

Scooby thought for a moment. Then he had an idea.

"Rollow re!" he barked. He ran down the aisle and disappeared.

"Where is he going?" Mrs. Howard asked.

"I think I know," Shaggy said. He led the others to the cooking department.

Scooby was standing in the demonstration kitchen. On the counter in front of him was an assortment of snacks arranged into words. They read, *Happy Birthday Shaggy!*

"Like, do I have the greatest pal in the world or what?" Shaggy asked.

"Rooby-Dooby-Doo!" barked Chef Scooby.

About the Author

As a boy, James Gelsey used to run home from school to watch the Scooby-Doo cartoons on television (only after finishing his homework). Today, he still enjoys watching them with his wife and two daughters. He also has a real dog named Scooby who loves nothing more than a good Scooby Snack!

EXCLUSIVE HINTS & TIPS

CARTOON NETWORK®

SCOOBY-DOO!

Classic Creep Capers

Here's our plan...

Relp!

Scooby-Doo™ Classic Creep Capers Game Clue Hints and Tips for Nintendo 64

To find the secret stash of Scooby Snacks in the 3rd episode, drop the banana peel in front of the Witch Doctor in the jungle trails. To build up courage, find the kitchen in each episode and stack a Shaggy sandwich. For a special surprise, collect all of the clues in any level. Look for Velma's glasses in the Egyptian Wing of the Museum in the first episode. Watch out for monsters! They will make your courage meter go down.

Scooby-Doo™ Classic Creep Capers Game Clue Hints and Tips for Game Boy Color

Repair the stool, then use it to get a light bulb from a broken fixture in Dr. Jekyll's lab. To fool the mad scientist, use the label maker and label tape to spell DNA. Then use the label on the bottle marked Cow Extract. To escape from the basement and find a missing clue, you must eat all of the cheese blocking the door.

NINTENDO.64

coming soon

SCOOBY-DOO and all related characters and elements are trademarks of Hanna-Barbera © 2000. CARTOON NETWORK and logo are trademarks of Cartoon Network © 2000. PlayStation and the PlayStation logos are registered trademarks of Sony Computer Entertainment Inc. Nintendo, Nintendo 64, the "N" logo, Game Boy and Game Boy Color are trademarks of Nintendo of America Inc. All rights reserved. THQ and the THQ logo are trademarks of THQ Inc.